S0-ABD-355

Dear Parents and Educators,

Welcome to Penguin Young Readers! As parents and educators, you know that each child develops at his or her own pace—in terms of speech, critical thinking, and, of course, reading. Penguin Young Readers recognizes this fact. As a result, each Penguin Young Readers book is assigned a traditional easy-to-read level (1–4) as well as a Guided Reading Level (A–P). Both of these systems will help you choose the right book for your child. Please refer to the back of each book for specific leveling information. Penguin Young Readers features esteemed authors and illustrators, stories about favorite characters, fascinating nonfiction, and more!

Clara and Clem Under the Sea

LEVEL **1**

GUIDED READING LEVEL **C**

This book is perfect for an **Emergent Reader** who:
- can read in a left-to-right and top-to-bottom progression;
- can recognize some beginning and ending letter sounds;
- can use picture clues to help tell the story; and
- can understand the basic plot and sequence of simple stories.

Here are some **activities** you can do during and after reading this book:
- Making Predictions: Sometimes, pictures contain clues in them that can help you guess what will happen next. On each spread, there is a clue about what animal Clara and Clem will see next. Have the child go through the story, find the clues, and try to guess what animal is coming!
- Rhyming Words: On a separate piece of paper, make a list of all the rhyming words in this story. For example, *fair* rhymes with *there*, so write those two words next to each other.

Remember, sharing the love of reading with a child is the best gift you can give!

—Bonnie Bader, EdM
　Penguin Young Readers program

*Penguin Young Readers are leveled by independent reviewers applying the standards developed by Irene Fountas and Gay Su Pinnell in *Matching Books to Readers: Using Leveled Books in Guided Reading*, Heinemann, 1999.

To Katie and her new adventure.
With love. xoxo Dad

PENGUIN YOUNG READERS
Published by the Penguin Group
Penguin Group (USA) LLC, 375 Hudson Street, New York, New York 10014, USA

USA | Canada | UK | Ireland | Australia | New Zealand | India | South Africa | China

penguin.com
A Penguin Random House Company

Copyright © 2014 by Ethan Long. Published by Penguin Young Readers, an imprint
of Penguin Group (USA) LLC, 345 Hudson Street, New York, New York 10014.
Manufactured in China.

Library of Congress Cataloging-in-Publication Data is available.

ISBN 978-0-448-47812-8 (pbk)   10 9 8 7 6 5 4 3 2 1
ISBN 978-0-448-47813-5 (hc)   10 9 8 7 6 5 4 3 2 1

Clara and CLEM Under the Sea

by Ethan Long

Penguin Young Readers
An Imprint of Penguin Group (USA) LLC

8

11

A big, big saw.

19

26

That is

The End!